Disney's DuckTales

Silver Dollars for Uncle Scrooge

By Gina Ingoglia
Illustrated by Willy Ito

A Golden Book • New York
Western Publishing Company, Inc., Racine, Wisconsin 53404

Library of Congress Catalog Card Number: 87-82723 ISBN: 0-307-07055-7
MCMXCI

Huey had an idea.

"Uncle Scrooge's birthday is tomorrow. Let's give him a surprise party."

"We'll need lots of ice cream and cake," said Dewey.

"And flowers to make the house look nice," said Louie. "What kind would Uncle Scrooge like?"

"Maybe my book on dried flowers will help," said Mrs. Beakley.

"Let's get those," said Dewey, laughing, as he pointed to *Silver Dollars*. "Uncle Scrooge is the richest duck in the world. He'll love flowers named after money."

The little ducks called Scrooge's friends.
"Everybody can come," said Webby. "It will be a great party."

They went to the store to buy
party hats,
cake mix,
ice cream,
and a big bunch of silver dollars.

On the way home Dewey lost the shopping list.

A few minutes later Flintheart Glomgold, the world's second richest duck, found it.

"Silver dollars," he read. "A *big bunch* of them! That sounds like lots of money. I think I'll go to that party and take them for myself. I'll get the Beagle Boys to help me."

for Uncle Scrooge's party tomorrow—
① PARTY HATS
② CAKE MIX
③ ICE CREAM
④ BIG BUNCH OF SILVER DOLLARS

Huey and Louie got right to work. They baked
a huge birthday cake. When it was cool, they
frosted it with green icing.

"Green is Uncle Scrooge's favorite color," said
Huey, licking his sticky fingers.

"That's because it's the color of dollar bills,"
said Louie, laughing.

Dewey and Webby set the table and put party hats at each place.

"The silver dollars look nice," said Webby.

"It's lucky that Uncle Scrooge is away and won't be back until tomorrow," said Dewey. "He'll really be surprised!"

Meanwhile, at his mansion across town, Flintheart was busy talking to the Beagle Boys.

"I don't know how big the bunch will be. Just carry as much as you can," he said.

"Don't worry, boss," said Big Time. "We'll get all the money."

The next afternoon the party guests arrived.
Launchpad McQuack and Doofus were first.
Gyro Gearloose hurried up the walk with
Gladstone Gander right behind him.

Quacky McSlant was just in time. "Scrooge's
car is coming down the street!" he said.

They all hid and waited for Scrooge. When the
bell rang, Duckworth opened the door.

"Good afternoon, sir," he said, trying not to
smile.

Scrooge stepped into the room.

"SURPRISE!" everybody shouted. "Happy
birthday, Uncle Scrooge!"

"Excuse me, sir," said Duckworth. "Look who I found whispering outside. It seems they've come to take your bunch of silver dollars."

"Silver dollars!" said Scrooge with a big smile. "Where are they?"

Dewey laughed. "It's a mistake," he said. "The silver dollars aren't money. They're dried flowers."

"Flowers!" snorted Flintheart. "They're not worth anything at all!"

"You're wrong, Glomgold," said Scrooge. "There's nothing more valuable than having my friends and family remember me on my birthday."

He put his arms around the little ducks and added, "Especially when it's a surprise!"